THE SUBURBAN JUNGLE

Rough Housing

by John "The Gneech" Robey

I0647496

Suburban Jungle (Rough Housing)
Volume One: Giant Enemy Crab!

To Kerry and Frostdemn. Vaya con Dios.

SORRY MS. MANAGER, BUT I'VE GOT CUSTOMERS!

YOUR OFFICE IS BACK THAT WAY.

IT'S EASY TO SPOT. IT SAYS "MANAGER" ON THE DOOR.

RIGHT.

HUSHED MEETINGS BOOTH

RESERVED -no shanking-

Manage Offic

UM... EXCUSE ME?

CRASH

!

POMF!

WAHAA!!!

THAT HORRIBLE, GARISH MONSTROSITY-- IT'S MY CURSE!

WAIT!

MY UNCLE SAID THERE'S A LIVE-IN APARTMENT FOR THE MANAGER...

DO YOU KNOW WHERE IT IS?

SORRY-- I DIDN'T KNOW IT WAS A PAINFUL SUBJECT.

I... I'LL JUST GO. *SOB*

SURE, IT'S JUST THROUGH THAT DOOR...

...BUT THE THING IS...

LANNNGLEEEEYYY!!!

YOU DON'T KNOW ABOUT THE FRIDAY NIGHT RUMBLE?

...NO...?

DUDE! IT'S, LIKE, TOTALLY THE ROUGH HOUSE'S *THING!*

BRAWLS USED TO BREAK OUT ON FRIDAY NIGHT SO REGULARLY, THEY JUST WENT AHEAD AND MADE IT AN EVENT AND ADDED A COVER CHARGE!

WHIMPER

GIVEN HOW DEAD THE PLACE IS EVERY OTHER NIGHT, IT'S PROBABLY THE ONLY THING THAT'S KEPT 'EM IN BUSINESS.

I THINK I FEEL ANOTHER PRIMAL SCREAM MOMENT COMING ON.

WHAAAAAAT?

WHY HAVEN'T THE COPS SHUT THE PLACE DOWN???

YOU'RE NEW TO MISSING KEYS, AREN'T YOU?

WHAT DO YOU MEAN?

DUDE.

DUDE!

DUDE?

DUUUUUDE.

(*PRONOUNCED "KHAN-*GRAY*-HO" -ED.)

WELL, IT'S LIKE I SAID, IF THE HOTEL'S A WASH, I'LL JUST KNOCK IT DOWN AND SELL THE LAND.

I'VE ALREADY HAD AN OFFER FROM MORRISON MONKEY.

OH.

BUT... WHAT ABOUT THE STAFF?

THEY'LL JUST HAVE TO FIND OTHER JOBS, I GUESS.

NO, YOU DON'T UNDERSTAND, UNCLE LEONARD. THEY LIVE HERE! THEY--

blink   *blink*

THEY DO *WHAT?*

THEY, UH, *PRACTICALLY* LIVE HERE. EVERYONE ELSE LEFT...

BUT PARKER, LANGLEY, BOUNCE, AND RUFO STAYED.

THERE MUST BE A REASON.

WELL THAT'S NICE, BUT I'M NOT RUNNING A CHARITY... UH... CHARITY.

IF THE PLACE IS REALLY AS BAD AS YOU SAY, IT'S GOTTA GO!

WAIT!

...WAIT?

LET ME FIX IT, UNCLE LEONARD.

"FIX IT?"

I CAN FIX IT! JUST GIVE ME SOME TIME!

AND...

...I MIGHT NEED A LITTLE MORE MONEY. MAYBE...

ULP

...MAYBE A *LOT* MORE MONEY.

CHARITY...

...

OKAY, TELL YOU WHAT. TAKE A FEW DAYS, AND MAKE TWO LISTS.

ON ONE LIST, WRITE DOWN EVERYTHING GOOD ABOUT THE PLACE AND WHY IT SHOULD STAY OPEN.

ON THE OTHER LIST, PUT DOWN EVERYTHING THAT NEEDS FIXING.

YES! YES, I'LL DO THAT. THANK YOU UNC--

"BECAUSE THE STAFF NEED THEIR JOBS" DOESN'T QUALIFY AS A GOOD ENOUGH REASON.

GOT IT?

...OH. UM, RIGHT. GOT IT.

OKAY. I'LL CALL YOU NEXT WEEK.

OKAY. THANK YOU, UNCLE LEONARD.

BEEP!

OH BOY...

THE SUBURBAN JUNGLE
ROUGH HOUSING

ISSUE 3

by John "The Gneech" Robey

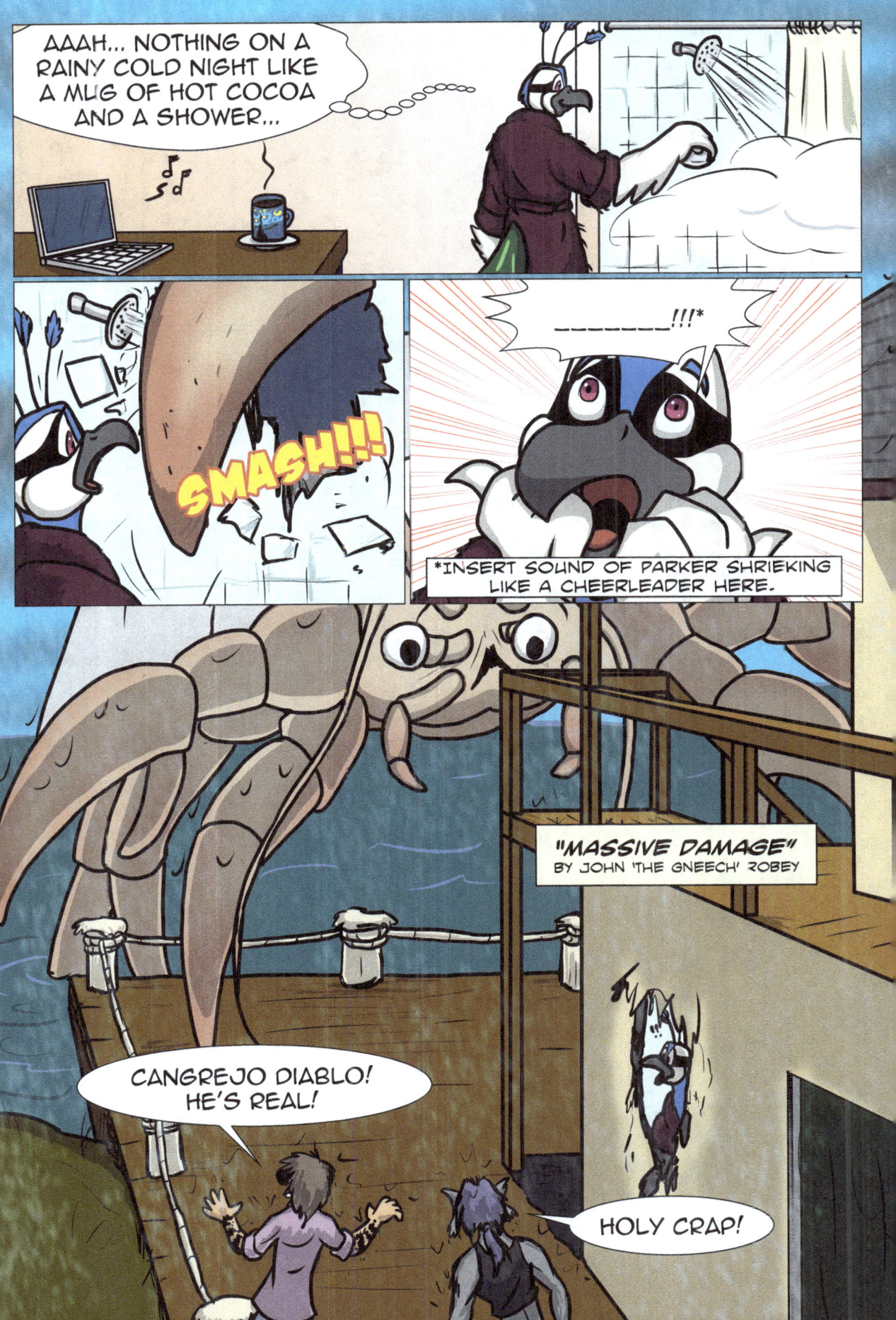

GET *YOU?* WHAT DO YOU MEAN?

CANGREJO DIABLO DRAGG'D MY SHIP UNDER- I WAS THE ONLY SURVIV'R! NOW 'E'S 'ERE TO FINISH THE JOB!

YOU MEAN THE ONLY REASON HE'S ATTACKING THE HOTEL IS TO GET TO YOU?

AYE, CURSE 'IM!

BOOT!

SLAM!

NO! YOU CAN'T *DO* THIS T' ME!

BAM! BAM! BAM! BAM!

HAAAALLLP!!!

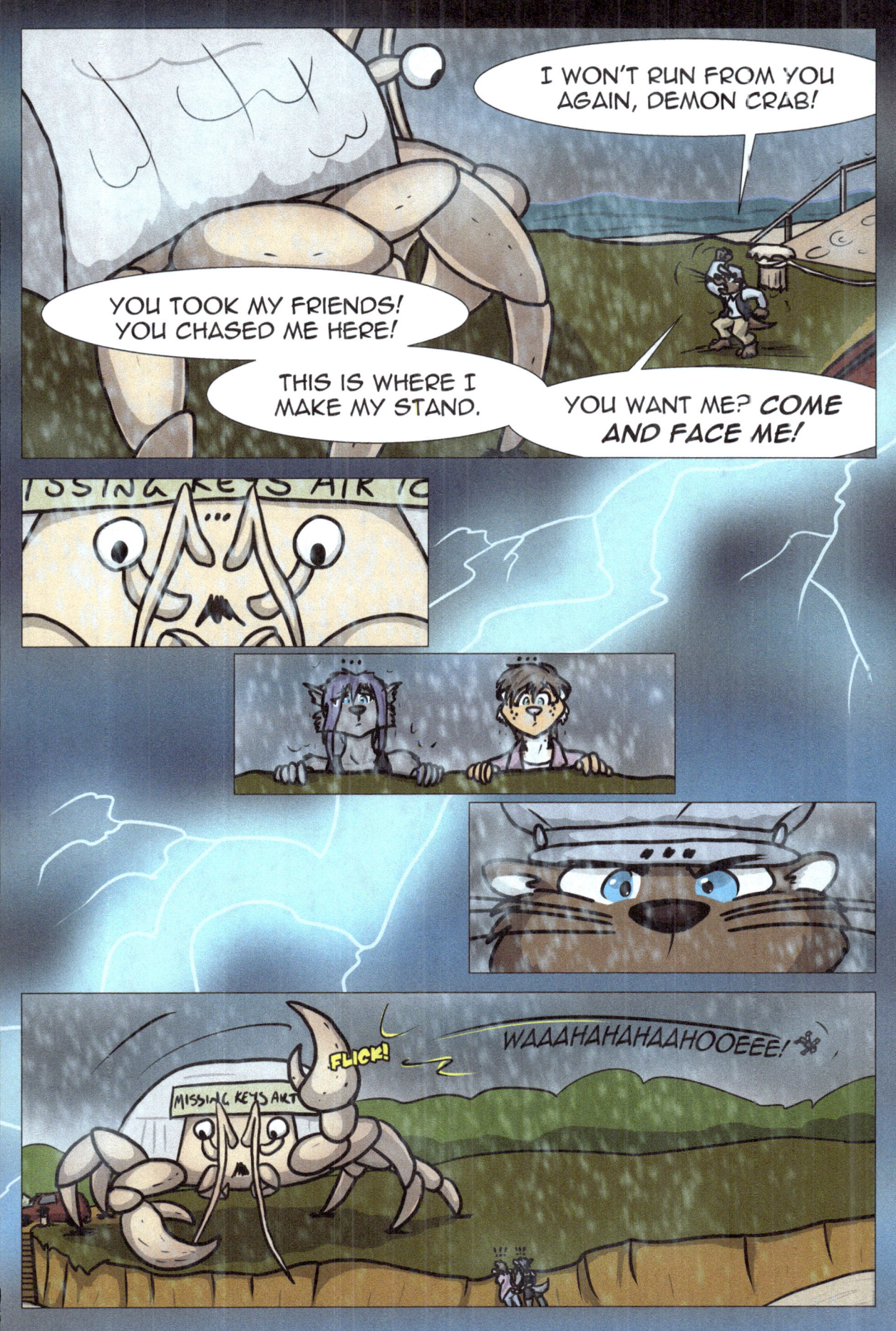

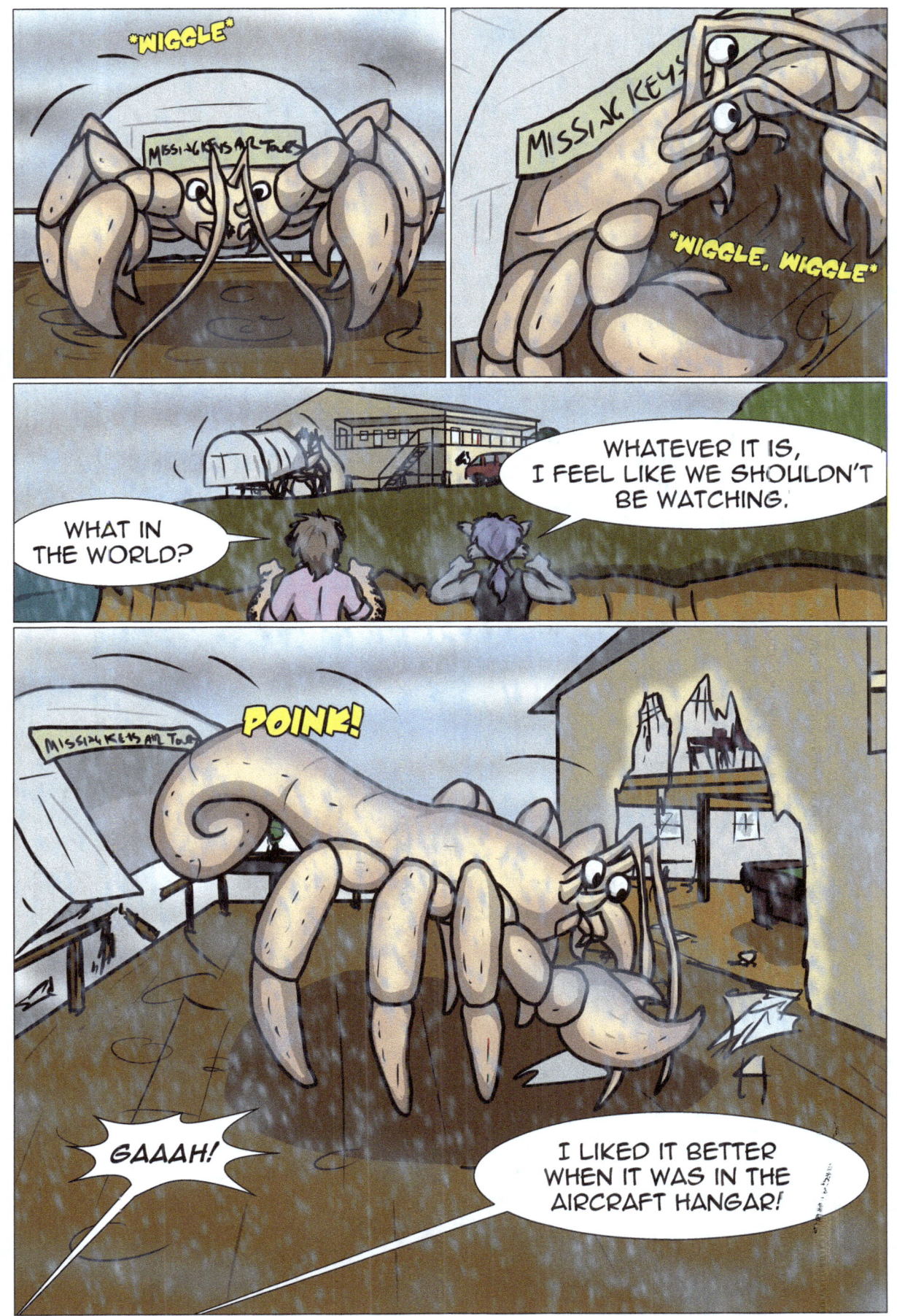

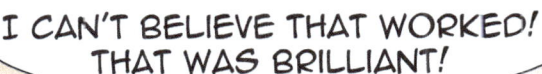

I CAN'T BELIEVE THAT WORKED! THAT WAS BRILLIANT!

WHAT I WANT TO KNOW IS WHERE WE WERE SUPPOSED TO FIND A STEAMER WITH 150,000 GALLON CAPACITY.

WHAT *I* WANNA KNOW IS WHAT WAS THAT CRACK ABOUT YOUR UNCLE KNOCKING DOWN THE ROUGH HOUSE!

WELL, JUST WHAT I SAID. MY UNCLE SAYS IF THE PLACE IS TOO MUCH TROUBLE, HE'S GOING TO KNOCK IT DOWN AND SELL THE LAND.

I'VE GOT A WEEK TO CONVINCE HIM NOT TO.

AND YOU DIDN'T *TELL* US THIS? GEEZE, MANAGER, YOU'RE NO BETTER THAN BOSLEY WAS!

HEY, LANGLEY, COME ON. SHE JUST RISKED HER NECK TO SAVE THIS PLACE FROM CANGREJO DIABLO.

WEEKLY WEIRD NEWS

The Monster is Real!

The Attack of Cangrejo Diablo! p. 1

Mystery Figure Controls the Fate of Dozens!

Who is the enigmatic "Uncle Leonard" and what does he want? p. 21

All of these stories and more can be found in The Suburban Jungle

www.suburbanjungle.com

THE SUBURBAN JUNGLE
ROUGH HOUSING

Issue 4

by John "The Gneech" Robey

YOU DIDN'T KNOW? RUFO'S WON THE PAST TWO YEARS IN A ROW.

REALLY? AWESOME! THAT'S THE FIRST $5,000 IN THE BAG!

WHOA, HOLD UP THERE, MANAGER. THAT $5,000 IS 50% OF MY INCOME FOR THE YEAR!

NOT IF WE CAN GET THE ROUGH HOUSE UP AND RUNNING PROPERLY AGAIN!

GETTING PEOPLE PAID IS ONE OF MY TOP PRIORITIES!

PFFT.

LIKE WE'RE GONNA FALL FOR *THAT* AGAIN.

HUH?

SO LET ME GET THIS STRAIGHT...

Friday Night Rumble FUNDRAISER! Cover Charge $20 Bring your own chairs Facesmashing free

BLAP!

CRUNCH!

AFTER WORKING HERE WITH NO PAY IN EXCHANGE FOR A ROOM, YOU WANT ME TO WIN $5,000 AND TURN IT OVER TO THE BAR FOR YOU?

UH... WELL... YEAH, I GUESS IT DOES SOUND PRETTY BAD WHEN YOU PUT IT THAT WAY.

I'M SORRY. FORGET I SAID ANYTH–

SURE, I'LL DO IT.

BUT YOU GOTTA DO SOMETHING FOR ME.

HEY... THAT JUDGE IS DREZZER WOLF! I KNOW THAT GUY!

Rainforest Talent Agency
Finding the Beautiful People Since 1987

OOH, YOU LUCKY GIRL! INTRODUCE US?

SERIOUSLY? HE'S OLD ENOUGH TO BE YOUR FATHER.

WHO CARES HOW OLD HE IS? HE'S A JUDGE! THAT GIVES US AN *IN*!

HEY! HEY! DREZZLER WOLF! OVER HERE!

THAT'S "DREZZER." THERE'S NO L IN IT.

'ELLO, YES? OH! CHARITY! WHAT ARE YOU DOIN' 'ERE?

HI, UNCLE DREZZER!

"UNCLE"...?

I WASN'T EXPECTING TO SEE YOU IN MISSING KEYS. AND IN A BIKINI, NO LESS!

YOU LOOK SO MUCH LIKE YOUR MOTHER DID AT THAT ASE.

WE'RE DOING A COMMUNITY EVENT ON THE BEACH!

YOU MIGHT HAVE PUT UP A SIGN.

AHEH... YEAH, PROBABLY SHOULD HAVE. BUT I THOUGHT BOUNCE WAS HERE? HE SHOULD HAVE LET YOU IN.

NOBODY ANSWERED WHEN I KNOCKED.

BUT IT DOESN'T MATTER NOW.

CHARITY, THIS IS MORRISON MONKEY.

HE'S INTERESTED IN BUYING THE PROPERTY.

BUT UNCLE LEONARD! I TOLD YOU I'D RAISE THE $10,000...

CHARITY, WHERE ARE YOU GOING TO FIND $10,000 LYING AROUND?

I DON'T WANT YOU TAKING OUT A CRAZY LOAN OR ANYTHING LIKE THAT.

IT'S NOT A LOAN! THE WHOLE TEAM IS PULLING TOGETHER TO EARN--

LEONARD, CAN WE GET ON WITH THIS, PLEASE?

I HAVE A LOT OF OTHER PROPERTIES STILL TO LOOK AT THIS AFTERNOON.

YES OF COURSE, SORRY.

CHARITY, LET US IN, PLEASE.

AS YOU CAN SEE, WE'VE GOT PLENTY OF ROOMS READY FOR GUESTS.

IF ONLY YOU HAD SEVERAL GUESTS READY FOR ROOMS.

WE'RE WORKING ON IT!

THAT'S WHY THE STAFF IS AT THE COMMUNITY EVENT!

WE'RE BUILDING THE BUSINESS!

IT'S A WASTE OF TIME.

THIS HOTEL IS A COMPLETE FAILURE. I INTEND TO BULLDOZE IT TO SIX INCHES OF TOPSOIL AND BUILD AN ENTIRE NEW RESORT HERE.

IT'S... IT'S NOT A WASTE OF TIME.

LET'S GET ON WITH IT. I WANT TO SEE THE BEACHFRONT ACCESS.

...

SORRY ABOUT THAT, MORRISON. THANKS FOR YOUR PATIENCE.

WELL IT'S JUST ABOUT EXHAUSTED. I'M GOING NOW.

OF COURSE. I'LL CALL YOU TOMORROW.

AS FOR YOU, YOUNG LADY, YOU'D BETTER GET BACK TO THAT CONTEST.

AND TELL DREZZ I SAID, "HEY."

WHAT'S THE POINT IF YOU'RE SELLING THE HOTEL...?

HE HASN'T MADE ME ANY OFFERS, YET.

COME BACK WITH $10,000, AND WE'LL DISCUSS IT.

ZOOM!!!

Pssht...

GUYS! GUYS! I'M *SO* SORRY!

WELL, LOOK WHO COULD BE BOTHERED TO SHOW UP!

MY UNCLE SHOWED UP AT THE ROUGH HOUSE.

WE'VE *REALLY* GOT TO WIN THIS THING!

YOUR HOTEL-OWNING UNCLE, YOU MEAN? NOT JUDGE HOTTIE OVER THERE?

YEAH, OKAY, THAT COUNTS AS URGENT.

HOW'S IT GOING? WHAT ARE OUR CHANCES?

HONESTLY...?

WE GOTTA LOTTA COMPETITION, MANAGER!

SERIOUSLY. IT'S STUDS AND BABES AS FAR AS THE EYE CAN SEE!

THIS CALLS FOR DESPERATE MEASURES!

EH???

HUH? WHAT 'MEASURES'?

I'LL SLEEP WITH AS MANY JUDGES AS IT TAKES TO WIN!

GET BACK HERE.

WOW... JUST... WOW!

PARKER, YOU WERE AMAZING!

GHEE HEE HEE

AND BOUNCE! WHY DIDN'T YOU TELL ME YOU WOULD ENTER?

YOU DIDN'T ASK.

ALL RIGHT, THANK YOU EVERYONE! WE'VE TALLIED UP THE VOTES.

AND THE WINNERS ARE...

FIRST FOR YOU AGAIN, I BET.

BACK TO THE KITCHEN FOR ME.

SORRY, CHICA.

FIRST PRIZE... BOUNCE OTTER!

BOUNCE???

HEH.

FIRST RUNNER-UP, PARKER PEACOCK. SECOND RUNNER-UP, TYRONE TIGER...

NOT EVEN... TOP THREE...?

SORRY, AMIGO.

KEEP IT. YOU EARNED IT. AND YOU'LL NEED IT.

UNCLE LEONARD?

CHARITY, LET ME TELL YOU SOMETHING.

WHEN I WAS 29, MY LIFE WAS A COMPLETE MESS. I WAS DIVORCED, DEPRESSED, AND WORKING IN A CORNER BAR THAT THE OWNER WANTED TO SELL.

TO SAVE MY JOB, I TOOK WHAT LITTLE SAVINGS I HAD AND USED IT AS THE DOWN PAYMENT TO BUY THE PLACE.

IT WAS A HUGE GAMBLE.

BUT IT PAID OFF, BECAUSE I PUT EVERYTHING I HAD INTO IT.

NOW THE ROUGH HOUSE? IS A COMPLETE MESS.

I'D GO SO FAR AS TO SAY IT'S AN UTTER DISASTER.

NNF.

I HAD NO IDEA JUST HOW MUCH OF A MESS IT REALLY WAS WHEN I BOUGHT IT.

BUT THE THING IS...?

THAT'S ALL ON ME, CHARITY. NOT YOU.

THIS IS IT, CHARITY CHEEGER!

THIS IS YOUR BIG CHANCE TO PROVE YOURSELF...

AS MANAGER OF UNCLE LEONARD'S NEW HOTEL!

Missing Keys, California
The Rough House
Hotel • Bar • Surf Shop

THIS IS THE END... OF THE BEGINNING...

...OF THE BEST TIME OF YOUR LIFE!

NEW SIGN LOOKS PRETTY GOOD, DOESN'T IT?

IT REALLY DOES. I CAN'T THANK YOU ENOUGH, ROXIE!

SURE YOU CAN! LET'S DO THAT DATE AROUND MISSING KEYS AGAIN.

ONLY PROPERLY, NOW THAT YOU AREN'T FREAKING OUT ABOUT THE ROUGH HOUSE.

OKAY, DEAL! IT'S FUNNY, THO-- THE WAY YOU KEEP SAYING "DATE" ALMOST MAKES IT SOUND LIKE YOU'RE HITTING ON ME. HEH!

PFFT. DON'T BE SILLY.

I'M *TOTALLY* HITTING ON YOU!

...AAAND MAYBE THE WEIRDEST....?

NEXT ISSUE: "READY TO RUMBLE!"

The Rough House presents... **ASK THE CAST!**

"SO WHAT HAVE YOUR FOLKS AND AUNTS AND UNCLES BEEN UP TO SINCE LAST TIME WE SAW THEM?"

"EVERYONE IN GOOD HEALTH, I HOPE?"

WELL I WASN'T EVEN BORN WHEN THE LAST SJ STORY ENDED, SO I DON'T KNOW WHAT THEY WERE DOING LAST TIME YOU SAW THEM.

BUT I CAN TELL YOU WHAT THEY'RE DOING NOW!

DAD INVENTED A SEARCH-ALGORYTHM-THINGIE AND SOLD IT TO BOOGLE FOR A PILE OF CASH. NOW HE WRITES SILLY GAMES FOR SMARTPHONES.

MOM TEACHES FRENCH AND GERMAN AT A HIGH SCHOOL.

AUNT TIFFANY IS STILL A MOVIE STAR, OF COURSE. UNCLE LEONARD INVESTS HER MONEY INTO REAL ESTATE, LIKE THE ROUGH HOUSE!

UNCLE LOUIS DRAWS WEB-COMICS ABOUT HAIRLESS APES, CALLED "FLESHIES." IT'S... KINDA WEIRD.

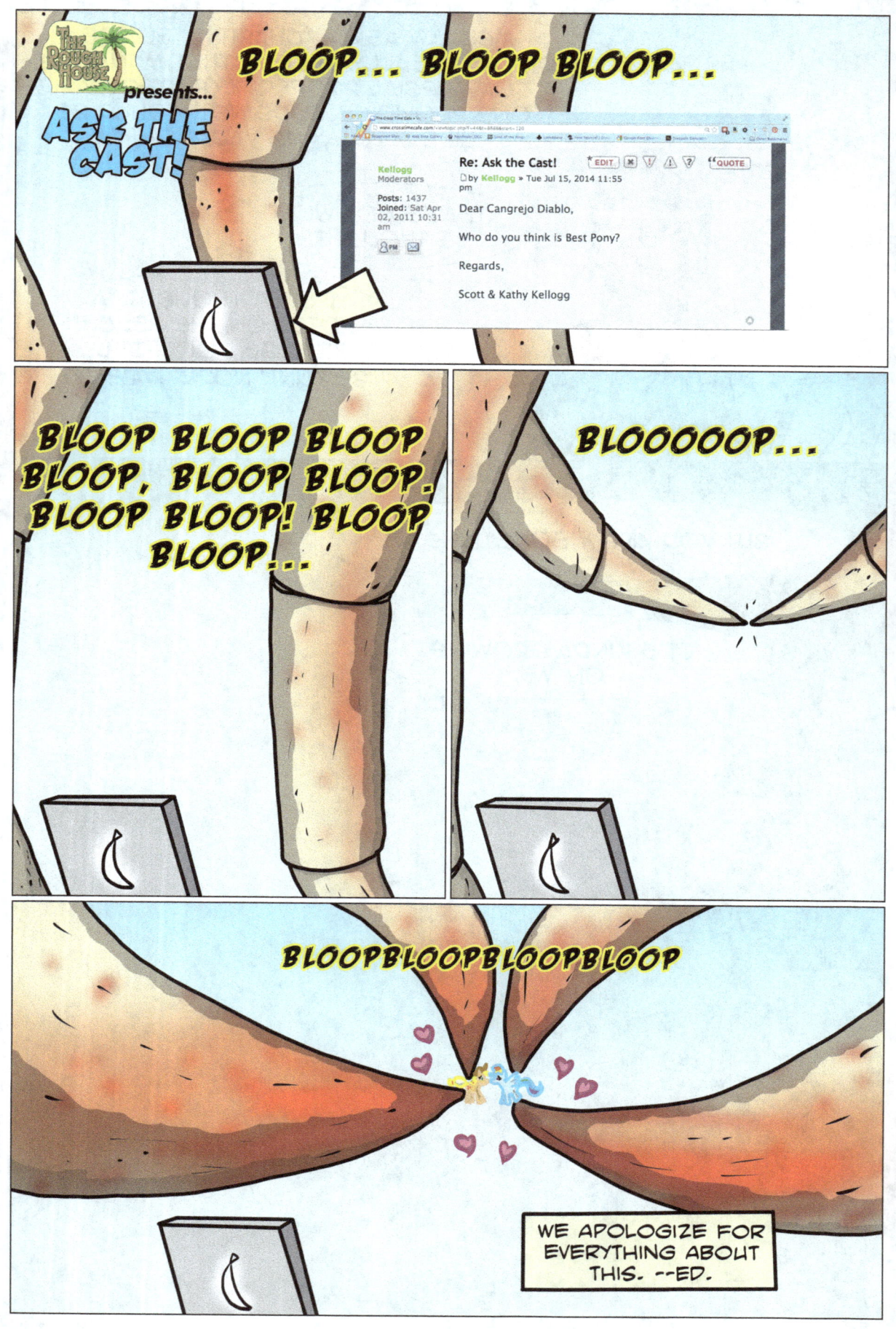